Submerged

Garrie Fletcher

First Published in the UK in 2019 by Mantle Lane Press

Copyright © Garrie Fletcher 2019

The right of Garrie Fletcher to be identified as author of this work has been asserted by him.

This book is sold subject to the condition that it shall not, by the way of trade or otherwise, be lent, resold, hired out, or otherwise circulated without the publisher's prior consent in any form of binding or cover other than that in which it is published and without a similar condition, including this condition, being imposed on the subsequent purchaser.

ISBN 978-1-9998416-8-3

Mantle Lane Press
Springboard Centre
Mantle Lane
Coalville
LE67 3DW
www.mantlelanepress.co.uk
www.mantlearts.org.uk

Printed and bound in the UK by
Imprint Digital, Upton Pyne, Exeter, EX5 5HY

Cover illustration by Jessamy Hawke
www.jessamyhawke.co.uk

For my children.

Submerged

The Captain says we should keep looking, but I've had enough. When I tell him I'm going to kill myself, he sulks.

"You're giving in? A man under my command? it's…"

"It's enough," I tell him. "I'm an old man."

The Captain stares at me with his unblinking eyes.

"You're old too," I say. "The paintwork on your uniform is faded and scuffed, and that arm of yours has never been the same since I dropped you." I look away. The Captain may only be twenty centimetres tall, but he can look down on you. I leave him on the platform and walk into the ticket office.

In the waiting area are red plastic bucket seats on metal frames. The first one I sit on snaps off when I put my weight on it. The second holds. I stretch my legs out in front of me and let the miles throb out through my calves and heels. The train station, like everywhere else, has started to be reclaimed by the earth. The paint has peeled away to reveal cracked plaster, and, behind the glass of the ticket office, a small tree is growing through the collapsed ceiling towards a large hole in the roof. I've been to London once since everybody disappeared. The dogs are worse there and hunt in large packs. It was there that I dropped the Captain running across Trafalgar Square.

"You're going to do it?" Bunny, her voice muffled.

I open the top flap of the backpack and let her head poke out.

"You're going to do it?"

Bunny's voice is treacle compared to the granite of the Captain's. She's a dirty pink, her fur matted, and she's lost an ear, but she still sounds bright and optimistic.

"What about everybody else? What about the kids and Agnethe? You can't give up on them."

"There's nothing to give up on," I tell her.

Bunny's large brown eyes are a doorway to a better time. I pull the flap back over and buckle it tight.

There's a route planner in the corner that's still readable. I trace my finger along the line and read out the names like an invocation, "South Wigston, Narborough, Hinckley, Nuneaton, Coleshill Parkway, Water Orton, Birmingham New Street." I keep my finger pressed against Birmingham New Street until the tip goes numb.

That night, curled up tight in my sleeping bag and wedged in the corner of the office, I dream of the sea and the rhythmic 'ping' of sonar. Since returning to the Midlands, this has become a regular feature of my dreams - sea and sonar. These sounds remind me of black and white war films and long conversations with my grandfather, the gas fire hissing in the background. He served in submarines during the Second World War and only spoke about it towards the end of his life - it had taken him that long to find the words. In my dream I am on the East Coast, Lowestoft maybe, walking over the dunes with the taste of hard-boiled egg in my mouth and salt in my eyes. I am alone, the beach deserted, and then slowly, above the crash of the waves, I can hear children laughing. They are nearby; I look around. A hedge, set back from the dunes, blocks my view, but I can see two kites flying in the sky. Their tails flick as their lines almost cross. Their strings pulled taut against the power of the wind lead down into a field beyond the hedge. I try to shout, but no sound comes. I hear laughter again, innocent, playful and unmistakably Lara and Milo. I try to force my way through the hedge, but it is a tangled mesh of hawthorn that cuts my hands and face. I move along it, desperate to find a gap where I can get through. The laughter increases. The kites are above me. I come to a wooden stile, not quite consumed by the hedge, and scramble my way through. I fall to the ground panting, drums beating in my ears, and look around. The field is empty. I get to my feet. The kites continue their elaborate dogfight, nipping at each other's tails, but instead of being guided by the hands of my children it is merely the wind; their lines tangled in the bushes. I want to scream, but the world slips away leaving nothing but darkness and the electronic 'ping' of my grandfather's submarine.

In the morning, I sit on the platform with my legs dangling over the side.

"That dream again?" says the Captain standing where I left him last night. "It means something."

I ignore him and carry on eating from a can of cold baked beans.

"I get the bit about hearing your children. That makes sense. You're their father, of course, you miss them, but why the submarine?"

"Come on. We have a long way to go." I pick him up and place him in the big, front pocket of my camouflage jacket.

"Don't forget the lookout," orders The Captain.

I adjust the top flap on the rucksack so that Bunny can see out and then slip my arms through the straps.

We make good progress down the track from Nuneaton. Coleshill shouldn't take too long. The roads and motorways are virtually impassable. Tree roots have cracked the tarmac, and wild grass grows through the bodies of abandoned cars, but it's the dogs that stop us from using the roads unless necessary. The dogs are vicious and always hungry. The railways are untouched by nature, and the dogs stay away. It makes no sense at all, but then neither did all the people I'd ever cared about disappearing one day along with everyone else.

"Do you want to talk theories?" says The Captain.

"No."

"Leave him alone," says Bunny. "You know it annoys him."

"We need to keep him active and to stop all this talk of topping himself."

"Why would you say such a thing?" asks Bunny.

"You haven't told her then?" The Captain won't let it go.

I ignore him.

"I heard, but he doesn't mean it. Do you?" Bunny is pleading.

I ignore her.

"Genius here has come up with the perfect solution. The only thing he hasn't decided upon yet is how he's going to do it."

"Stop it, Captain. Stop it." Bunny is desperate

"That's why we're heading back to Birmingham," said The Captain. "To stop it."

Bunny doesn't speak again for ages. The Captain insists on whistling some inane pop tune that Lara loved. I clasp his head in my hand, but it's pointless. Soon, we're a long way from Nuneaton. I imagine it had been a pleasant enough place in its day, but now it's just a puzzle of brick, wood and metal-work that nature is slowly working its way through.

I've been walking the railways for years now and find it easy to fall into a rhythm using the sleepers as markers for my stride. Now and then I step out from between the tracks and walk alongside, the sound of the ballast under my boots like surf on the shingle, and I imagine I can taste the salt air.

"Is that it?" asks The Captain. "Is it the sound of these infernal grey stones that has you dreaming of the beach?"

"Leave him alone; he's thinking,"

Before everyone disappeared, things were normal. Agnethe and I were okay, and the kids were happy. They enjoyed school; their reports were good, and, more importantly, they had friends. I didn't see as much of them as I would have liked, but that was the same for everyone I knew. We were all working hard for a better life for our kids. Now, when I think of home, I find it hard to picture them. Bits of detail remain, and I focus on that, but I worry that if I saw them in a group, I wouldn't be able to pick them out. The chances of me bumping into a crowd, and them being in it, are zero, but I worry about it anyway. If I can't remember what they look like what kind of father am I? I hold onto the hope that if everyone can vanish, then there's a chance that they can reappear and that warms me for a while until I think about how much time has passed.

When it first happened, I kept a log. I took notebooks from a shop in Birmingham and a fistful of pens, and at the end of every day, I would write an entry. In the top left corner, I would print the date and to the right of that the time. At first, I was shocked at how weak my handwriting was, and I would print everything. Then, over time, my writing improved and evolved into a decent form - neater than anything I ever attained at school. I recorded my day in a cold factual style: the time I awoke, what I had to eat, whether I washed or shaved, how many miles covered, my starting point, destination and so on. Then one day, I flicked back through the book to see what I'd written only to find that there were gaps. Not just the odd day but whole months and years were missing.

I was in Scotland when I discovered it; I was standing on the Forth Bridge, staring down at the dark, violent water. The notebooks fluttered like desperate birds when I dropped them over the edge, pages feathering out. The urge to jump in after them almost overwhelmed me. That was some time ago. Since then I've travelled the length and breadth of the country. I know there's no one here, but I keep looking.

Today's a beautiful early Autumn day. Some of the leaves have started to turn, and there is a sharpness in the air. There are no sounds of dog. The sky is clear of birds with only a few stray wisps of cloud, and my mind wanders. I can hear The Captain and Bunny discussing me. I slowly fade them out and drift back to the day it all happened. It was a Wednesday. I was working nights, and I'd got in just as Agnethe was herding the kids. I made myself a cup of tea and sat at the kitchen table. Agnethe gave me the stare. The Swedish stare with a hint of Viking.

"Okay. I'm on it."

I went up to Milo's room and knocked on the door. No answer. I knocked again and went in. Comic books covered the floor near his bed, and a half-assembled Lego kit was on top of his bedside cabinet: three Storm Troopers and a vehicle. He was asleep or pretending to be. I shook him and told him to wake up. He groaned and made the usual excuses. Lara was in the shower and shouted, in her most scathing tone, that, yes, she was getting up. Back in the kitchen, Agnethe was preparing breakfast.

"I wish you were here more," she said.

"I know. I wish I were here more, but we need the money."

"The kids need a dad. I need a husband."

That hurt. I tried to remember the look on Agnethe's face when she said it. The line of her nose, the shape of her mouth, but there was nothing. I could remember the Swedish Stare but not this. I could remember the sound of her voice when she was disappointed, but not when she was happy, and when I tried to picture her, it lacked definition. I know I said something about my work, about how important it is, but I can't remember what. I can't remember what my job is.

We'd run out of milk, and a trip to the shop seemed a handy escape, and that was the last I ever saw of them.

"Have you worked it out yet?" says The Captain.

"Leave him alone," says Bunny. "He's trying to remember.

"I think I've worked it out." There's a hint of smugness in The Captain's voice.

"No, he hasn't. It'll be something silly again," says Bunny.

I can't tune them out this time.

The Captain continues, "It's a computer simulation. It has to be."

"Why?" I ask.

"Well, there are parts of your memories that you can't access, right?"

"Right."

"And there's parts of this world, that are very well defined and others that don't make sense."

"Such as?"

"The dogs. They never catch us. Even when you fell over that time and dropped me, we still managed to get away. And they only ever chase us towards places that we know and always toward the railway tracks. It's as if they're guiding us through here. Well, not guiding, guarding. They're securing the gaps, the parts of the programme that have become corrupted."

"So, I go out for milk one morning and get sucked into a computer programme?"

"No. You never got sucked in. You've always been in one. Only something has happened to it. Something has gone wrong. Do you remember that story you read about two tech billionaires who employed scientists to work out how to break us out of the computer simulation?"

I despair. This is the rubbish I have to put up with: alien abduction, zombie uprising, a flesh-eating virus that I'm immune to, a parallel universe that I've fallen into, and so on. Computer simulation is a new one though.

"What billionaires?" I ask.

"I can't remember," says The Captain

"Elon Musk?" offers Bunny. "Yes. That's it."

"Stupid name," says The Captain.

"Stupid theory more like," I say.

We cover a good fifteen miles or more and reach Coleshill Parkway before dark. The train station had been a modern single-story building that sat beneath the bridge that crossed the track. I have a memory of driving across the bridge, but I can't remember why. The once smooth red brick of the station has faded and cracked, and there are thin tendrils of bind-weed trying to take hold. I force the glass doors apart and sleep on the floor.

I'm on the beach again, sonar pinging in my ears. I hear children's laughter. I run over the dunes. The cold air stings my throat, and in the distance, I can see kites. I keep running. The dunes are unending. Milo and Lara are close enough to hear but impossible to see. I scream into the wind, lose my footing and tumble down a dune into a thick hedge. I try to untangle myself, to get back to the dunes, but I've rolled too far in. I can only go forward. I have to press on through the spikes and thorns that snag on my clothes and flesh. I shield my eyes with my arm as best I can, but it isn't long before blood is running into my eyes turning the whole world red. The laughter stops, and I fall out of the hedge into a field. I can hear the kites above me their plastic skins and tails snapping in the wind. And then the singing starts. Beautiful, sweet singing:

*"My daddy's dead.
My daddy's dead.
He's not right in the head.
My daddy's dead."*

I try to stand. I try to face them, to look at them, but a weight pushes me flat on the ground. I roll over and look up at the sky in time to see the kites diving down at me. I put my hands up, and the kites shatter against my arms spraying me with splintered wood and torn plastic. I look around, but no one is there. I hear the laughter fading, and then I spot the kite tails caught in the hedge. The tails untangle slowly from the spiky bush, and as I pull them through, I see something tied to each end. Both are postcard sized. I untie one and flip it over. On one side is a photograph of Agnethe and the kids. They are standing on a beach. The sun has caught their cheeks, and they are all smiling. On the back of the card, in my wife's handwriting, are the words: 'Our first holiday without Dad. Wish he were here.' I grab the other card and look at it. It is odd. It reminds me of the black and white Athena posters my sister had in the 80's. The image is high contrast with grainy, dramatic lighting, but instead of a muscular male model or a romantic couple, it's focus is an old man in bed. He looks familiar, but it isn't until I hear the electronic ping of sonar that I realise he looks like my grandfather. I turn the card over and try to read the writing on the back, but my eyes won't focus. I hold the card closer. Everything takes on the off-white shade of the card, and then nothing.

The next morning I wake up shivering. The sun isn't up. I go outside and feel my way around to the stairs that lead up to the footbridge over the track. I lay down and look up at the sky. A few stars are visible, and I wish I could name them. Their real names, not the ones I made up for the kids. The longer I lie there, the more stars I can see. We took a trip once, to the Lake District. We hired a remote cottage, and one night the four of us lay on the grass looking up at the sky. The kids fidgeted and moaned at first, saying it was boring, but as their eyes adjusted and as the stars came out, a beautiful calm came over them. That's how I felt then; as if those two moments were connected. I wasn't just lying on the floor of some shitty footbridge outside Birmingham. I was lying on the grass with my family in the Lake District. Both instances connected by the ancient light of stars.

The sky gradually warms through to a dark blue-violet, and the stars fade. The violet takes hold and moves into hot pink. A big grin spreads across my face. I can't ever remember seeing a morning like this. And then the growling starts.

The footbridge runs parallel with the road bridge; they are only three meters apart from each other. On the bridge opposite is a black, snarling mass of dogs. They must be standing on their hind legs, their heads poking above the side of the bridge, looking directly at me. In the whole time I've been alone, I've never been this close to a dog. The sun isn't fully up, but I can see their teeth, a nicotine yellow against the raw flesh of their mouths, and thick strands of saliva hanging from their jaws. I look around for my backpack and remember I've left it in the station. I run. I know I shouldn't have. I should have backed away slowly, but I can't, I have to get my bag. Everything I own in the world is in it including my last links to the kids. I reach the top of the steps and feel a thud vibrate through the footbridge. I look over my shoulder. A dog has leapt over. I jump down the first flight of stairs and hear three more thuds behind me. Shit, shit, shit. I drop down the next flight of stairs and ignore the sharp pain in my ankle. Without thinking, I throw myself over the side of the stairs, landing heavily on the tarmac, and knee myself in the mouth. I take a second and then roll over and run for the station entrance. Inside, I grab my bag and turn back towards the doors, but it's too late. The dogs are glaring at me, snarling, waiting.

"Use me," says Bunny.

I snatch her out of the backpack. "What do you mean?"

"You know what I mean."

"But, Bunny, I can't."

"You have to."

"If anyone is going to save us it should be me," says The Captain.

But Bunny is in my hand.

The dogs are moving closer, their bellies almost touching the floor, their eyes catching the reflected fire of the rising sun. I look at Bunny and feel nothing but shame.

"Do it," says Bunny.

"No!" shouts The Captain.

I throw her as high and as far as I can.

The dogs look up and follow her trajectory, craning their necks to see where she's going. At first, they do nothing. Then, as one, they turn and chase after her. I run back past the steps to the footbridge and out onto the platform, jump down onto the track, throw the backpack up onto the opposite platform and pull myself up after it. By the time the dogs notice, I am sat down catching my breath. They crowd along the first platform, barking and braying at me. A few of them peel away from the pack and go back up the stairs to the footbridge.

"Run!" shouts The Captain.

I pick up the backpack and drop down onto another stretch of track.

"Which way's Birmingham?"

"It's to the west of here," says The Captain. "Away from the sun."

I turn and run back under both bridges.

The dogs continue to chase alongside the track, but they won't come near it. Eventually, the verges become too overgrown for them to follow and we leave them behind.

The city's skyline is picked out by the morning sun. Not the expected sharp rectangular blocks, but with diffused edges. It isn't possible to pick out any detail from where I am, roughly five miles out, but it doesn't look right. To my left, as I trudge along the track, comes the sound of a river. The undergrowth beside the rails isn't too thick, and I manage to push my way through and dive in fully clothed. The water is freezing, and it leaves me gasping for air when I break the surface.

"Thanks a bunch," The Captain is not impressed.

"Sorry."

I take him out of my front pocket and place him on the grass to dry.

'Ping.'

"Did you hear that?" I look at The Captain.

"Of course I heard it."

'Ping.'

"Am I still asleep?"

"Pinch yourself."

I pull my sleeve back and grab my wrist until it hurts.

'Ping.'

"Where's it coming from?" says The Captain.

"Everywhere."

The sound is inside and outside my head and has exceptional clarity. There are no distortions from the wind or muffling from the bushes or trees. It is like being back in our old terraced house with the surround-sound system on, but better. I take my wet jacket off and hang it from a branch. The hairs on my arm stand up.

'Ping.'

The Captain, insists I am a sonar operator. I tell him to shut up.

The railway track leads us into the city and New Street Station. From the platform, I find my way up the stairs into the main concourse. The station is relatively unscathed, compared to others I've seen, with only a few wisteria and hydrangea climbing up the walls and escalators, and thin, pale grass growing through cracks in the floor. The once white spars and transparent over-head domes are covered in a weak green moss which gives the incoming light an olive tint and makes the vast vaulted space feel ancient and submerged. The Captain notes that our surroundings now befit our soundtrack - the pinging has not stopped. For a moment, I try to remember what it had been like. How the place had reverberated with people, their footsteps and overlapping conversations. Journeys terminating, crossing, intersecting, conjoining with glimpses of lives played out and gestures caught. The kids had come here with us when they were very young. No. They couldn't have. And yet I remember them running, desperate to catch a train.

I climb up the escalators and find padded seating. I lie down on it and try not to think about the sea as the ping of sonar drags me off to sleep.

The walk from the city centre along the railway line to my old house should be easy enough. I climb back down to the station and imagine I can smell hot, pungent dog. I drop onto the track that will lead me home through nearly a mile of tunnel. The Captain tells me it's an excellent spot for an ambush. I wait at the entrance of the tunnel and see no end to its darkness.

"You should run it. Get through it as quickly as possible."

"That's easy for you to say. I'll be doing all the running."

I empty my pack of everything except a very sharp machete, a bottle of water, and my torch. The discarded contents lie across the sleepers. It's a small collection of tins, maps, clothes and books. Impossibly, almost hidden by a pair of pants, is one of the journals I threw away in Scotland. I kick it hard and notice, as it flaps through the air, that its pages are blank.

"Don't worry," says The Captain. "I'll remember you."

"And how will you do that when I've gone?"

I run into the tunnel shouting as loudly as I can, the light from my torch flicking across the darkness. My voice echoes, amplified, ferocious, unstoppable. My limbs are thin and powerful. Years of walking has transformed me from fourteen stone to a wiry approximation of the man I was. The track curves ahead of me. My voice gives out, and the crunch of boots on gravel, like some demon snare-drum full of rocks, replaces my screams. Gradually a circle of light appears ahead, and I emerge from the tunnel at Fiveways, the edge of the city centre. I settle into a slower pace and then a steady walk. High walls of blue Victorian brick, flank the track. For the most part, these are clear of any vegetation. At the top, I can make out twisted sycamores and Boston ivy. I pass under a bridge, and the sonar pings shift pitch slightly, becoming higher and closer together. Maybe they're a tracking beacon? Perhaps this is what my dreams are trying to tell me all along: follow the sound. Behind me, comes the bark of dogs. I pick up the pace. They've never come onto the tracks before. The railway is safe. And yet now, now I can hear them behind me. I look back, but there is nothing to see. I move from a jog to a sprint. The ping shifts to a beep above the crunch of the gravel. All that matters is the running. My life will not end in the jaws of a dog.

The high brick walls give way to dense greenery. There is a canal that runs parallel with the track, but it's impossible to tell it's there. The barking grows louder. I push myself harder; air burns my throat, my calves start to tighten. Soon I'll be forced to stop. The University station is ahead, but the bridge over the track has collapsed blocking the way forward. I'm trapped. Behind me, the snarling intensifies. Around the bend in the track comes a mass of dogs, a tangled collection of legs and jaws howling at the air, their eyes fixed on me. Goldheart ivy, that looks like it's been splashed with yellow paint, and tree roots cover the collapsed bridge. Three sycamores are growing in the debris. I leap up and grab hold of the ivy. It snaps under my weight. I jump again, and this time a vine holds; I scramble up. The dogs attempt to follow me, but it is impossible. Instead, they stare up and growl in unison, a thick, mechanical sound that roots me to the spot. It is impossible to focus on one dog or to differentiate between breeds. My gaze slips over the dark, sleek fur, the crimson flesh and yellow teeth of their jaws. There is something beautiful in their vicious intent. Something humbling about their clarity of purpose: they want me dead, and nothing will stop them.

"Snap out of it man!" orders The Captain.

I look around. To the left, away from the station, the route is thick with sycamores and weeping willow. The road towards the station isn't as bad, and I can see a way through. A loud thud comes from below and then another. The dogs have used the rubble from the bridge to clamber onto the platform and are now ramming their collective weight against the glass doors that lead inside. I push on through the greenery. I have to get clear before they make their way through the station and up to me.

Westgate had been a large brick-paved area where people could park their cars, chain up their bikes, or catch a bus. The vegetation has not taken a firm hold here, and I can see the square beneath the pale grass that grows through the bricks. At the edge is a bike shed packed with bikes.

Home isn't far from here; twenty minutes walk at most. But, a bike would speed that up and make me a harder target for dogs, if the roads are passable. The shed has protected the bikes from the worst of the weather, and there is very little rust to be seen. The first one I try is chained, as is the second, but the third, a shabby mountain bike, only looks like it is chained up. When I pull it, the padlock pops open, and the bike comes free. I sit on it and put some pressure on the right pedal, ready to push off. The shattering of glass interrupts my preparations. I don't bother to look around. I push down on the pedal and frantically build up speed and skid left onto New Fosse Way. The road is surprisingly clear, apart from the rabid pack of dogs hurtling towards me. I hit the brakes and nearly go over the handlebars. There is only one way out now, towards the hospital. I look over my shoulder to see dogs from the station sweeping across the square, merging with the pack behind. I peddle as a man possessed and aim for the new hospital.

The kids were born here.

How could those moments, those sublime beginnings of our family story seem like fantasy, and this world of ravenous dogs and wild vegetation be all too real? It makes no sense at all.

The back tyre thuds against something hard and bursts, but I am not stopping. I skid out into the drop off point at the front of the hospital. Where once there had been sheets of glass and steel, curved lines and commanding columns, there are now flowering creepers, shattered glass, rusted metal and trees, lots of trees. Eucalyptus and willow surround the building, their roots dug deep beneath the fractured tarmac and cracked slabs, their branches growing into the sides of the floors above and clematis and weeds trail over everything.

The rear tyre disintegrates, and the bike slips from beneath me. Behind, I hear the dogs.

"Think man, think!" The Captain is frantic.

Broken windows look out from the hospital, but the ground floor remains intact and inaccessible. The revolving doors are dense with hazel leaving no way through.

"Is this it then?" says The Captain.

I pick up the bike and hurl it at the window next to the doors. It bounces off. I do it again and again.

"We've got to go. Or was this your plan all along? To be ripped to pieces."

I catch my breath, hold the bike over my head and throw it at the glass with all of my remaining strength. It shatters.

"Run!"

The dogs are streaming in from all angles, their snarling echoes around the campus.

I run across the entrance hall. A dull green light

covers the vast space. The last time I'd been here was with Agnethe and the kids, Lara needed a check-up; it was full of people. A painful howl erupts behind me as the dogs squeeze their way through the glass. I push open the doors to the stairs and then run up two steps at a time. I keep going until I get to the fifth floor. Once there, I grab whatever I can and throw it down the stairs: chairs, cabinets, plants, trolleys. I drag a large desk over from a reception area and block the doors. I weigh it down with as much furniture as I can move, and then I collapse exhausted. I don't realise I'm crying until The Captain says, "Steady on. We can regroup here and look at our options."

"What options? We don't have any options. Have you ever seen so many dogs? Have you ever seen dogs on the railway? This is messed up. We've been trudging around here for years, and as weird as all this shit is, we've never seen anything like this. All I wanted to do was to get home; to see our house one last time. To try and remember what it was like to be normal."

The Captain clears his throat. "It's no secret that I'm not keen on the whole suicide thing, but I respect your wishes. I'll do all that I can to help you through this. Sitting here sobbing is no use to anyone. You need to snap out of it. We need a base, somewhere secure; somewhere we can sleep and get our strength back. Now, get on your feet and find an office we can lock ourselves into for the night."

I find an office, collapse on the couch and sleep.

I am on the beach with sonar pinging in my ears and the laughter of children in the distance. The kites are fighting above the hedge, and the children, my children, can be heard giggling and talking behind it. I stop and listen. Their words are clear but incomprehensible to me. It is as if they are speaking another language. I try to call out, but no words come. The hedge bites and scratches me as I force my way through. I know it's pointless, but I have to try. I have to see their faces one last time. I fall through and land on the muddy ground. My breathing slowly calms, and the smell of damp soil fills my head. The distant sound of the sea recedes into a deep rumbling, like a car engine ticking over, only lower. I look up. In front of me sits a solitary dog. It's a thick, oily, black beast with powerful shoulders and slobbering jowls. It's no breed I've ever seen before, but there are hints of wolf, Rottweiler and something almost bear-like. The smell of dog is overpowering. I retch as if I'm going to be sick, but nothing comes up. I sit up and start to inch away. I push back into the hedge and look around for a way through. The hedge towers over me. On the dog's back is something, something dirty and pink: Bunny. She has an eye missing and has lost an arm, but she's managing to hold onto the leather collar around the dog's neck. The dog's breath is overpowering: rancid meat, foetid water and dried blood. Its powerful shoulders held high; its back legs turned out slightly displaying an angry erection. Then, they both begin to sing:

"My daddy's dead.
My daddy's dead.
He's not right in the head.
My daddy's dead."

I wake. The Captain is standing guard on the desk blocking the door. He hisses at me to be quiet. I sit back on the couch and listen. A sad, long, plaintive whine echoes through the building. There must be hundreds of dogs around the hospital, and yet they all remain quiet while this one dog sings.

"That's fucking terrifying."

"There's no need for language, Sir."

"Really? Not even now?"

"We have standards, Sir, and without those we're nothing."

"God, you're weird. What did my kids ever see in you?"

"Whatever you wanted them to."

I walk over to the window. It is still dark. I'd quickly got used to the lack of light at night when I was out in the countryside, but cities always give me the shivers. The night is clear, and the moon picks out the soft lines of buildings. I can make out the clock tower at the University of Birmingham, and, in the distance, the abstract blocks of the city proper. Where there should've been the glow of street lights and the amber rectangles of windows, there is nothing. Instead of the reassuring call of an ambulance or police car, there is only the disturbing wail of a dog singing into the night.

In the morning the sonar has returned. It has shifted in pitch again and is now a steady, almost familiar beep. I'd assumed my grandfather's time in submarines was the link to the sonar, but this was different. I know this sound.

"Are we safe, Captain?"

"Nothing to report, Sir."

I drag the desk away from the door and step out. The beeping gets louder.

"Can you hear that?"

"The beeping, Sir? Yes, it's been going throughout the night."

"Well, at least that bloody dog's stopped."

The corridor is empty; the floor is cold against my bare feet. The foyer runs around the edge of the building with two corridors leading off it at right angles. I peer around the corner of the first one. It is empty. I listen. I can hear sniffing in the distance. The beeping picks up the pace slightly. I walk into the next corridor, each footfall carefully balanced. The Captain reminds me that dogs rely more on their highly tuned sense of smell than they do on their hearing. The beeping gets faster. The next corridor is also empty, and I can hear no sounds of sniffing. Slowly, I work my way down it. The inside of the hospital is surprisingly untouched by the loss of cleaners, maintenance workers and the like, and looks pretty much as I remember it - apart from the lack of people. I stop. Goosebumps break out on my forearms. Turning slowly, I look back the way I've come. A silent pack of dogs block the mouth of the corridor. They are not growling or sniffing, but they are alert. Their ears are up and forward, their shoulders raised as if on tip-toe and I can make out their tails flicking from side to side. Their eyes are wide and fixed on me.

I start to edge backwards.

"I think you should check over your shoulder."

I don't remember putting The Captain in my pocket, but there he is.

At the other end of the corridor, about thirty meters away, is another pack of dogs.

To the left and the right of me are two doors, both labelled 'I.C.U.'

I turn to the door on the right and carefully open it.

The beeping becomes louder and faster.

"I've worked it out," says The Captain.

"What? How we can get out of here?"

"No. We can't get out of here."

"Cheers for that. I'm rescinding your promotion to morale officer."

"It's the beeping, Sir."

"Of course there's beeping. We're in a bloody hospital."

"Exactly!"

I push through onto the ward.

The ward is spotless. The beds are empty and freshly made. Despite it being daylight outside, the ward lighting is subdued and has the feel of dusk about it.

The beeping gets faster.

I walk past the beds and equipment: heart monitors, drips, screens, oxygen canisters on trolleys, clipboards with handwritten notes on, and stop at a light-box mounted on the wall. The box is on, and it flickers ever so slightly. On the glass screen is an x-ray of a skull. I stare at it. It doesn't look good. I'm sure I'm not a medical man, but the skull isn't right. There is a crack in the forehead, and the right eye socket is broken. Instinctively, I touch my eye and gently smooth my hand across my forehead. It feels fine.

"I think we need to go in there."

The Captain is looking at the door to another room.

"I don't want to go in there." My heart thuds in my chest.

"Come on, Sir. You have to do this. It's time to go home."

I am aware of pushing the door open and moving forward, but it is as if I am observing someone else do it.

Beep. Beep. Beep.

The dream-dog, the one I saw Bunny on, fills the room. Sat on its back legs it gazes into the distance. A cold, clinical light diffused around its massive head, and forelegs like downy tree trunks block my way. The smell of warm fur makes my head swim. Perspective skews, the scale all wrong. The dog towers above me. Its tongue hangs out the side of its mouth as it pants a mechanical rhythm. A pool of saliva forms on the floor. I hear Bunny's voice, sweet, reassuring. "It's okay to be afraid."

But I'm not.

I move forward into darkness. Fur surrounds me, thick, palpable black. Dry and yet fluid. When I was small, I was terrified of the dark, but this isn't like that.

It's comforting, safe, like a pet on a child's bed. There's a hand in mine, soft, gentle. The thumb makes slow circles on my palm, familiar, natural. All those miles. All that track. All those years.

"Did you think we'd leave you?"

"I…"

"Shush."

I'm floating in darkness, black, oily, fluid that engulfs me. I lose myself in it. Lose myself in the distant hiss of the sea.

I float up through the black, break the surface, and breathe.

Acknowledgements

Thanks to: the Tindal Street Fiction Group for workshopping an early draft of *Submerged* and letting me know I wasn't sinking; the Room 204 gang for their productivity; Peter Haynes for making me laugh like a drain; Juliet for putting up with my moods when I couldn't write; and Matthew Pegg and all at Mantle Lane for producing this great looking book.

This publication was supported using public funding by the National Lottery through Arts Council England

Mantle Lane Press would like to acknowledge support from Writing West Midlands.

Mantle Lane Press is a subsidiary of Mantle Arts Limited, which receives financial support from North West Leicestershire District Council.